# Lisa Penner-Dang

## My Monster DYSLEXIA and the Black Rock Crone of Dingle

Nightingale Books

NIGHTINGALE PAPERBACK



A CIP catalogue record for this title is
available from the British Library.

ISBN 978-1-78788-038-2

*Nightingale Books is an imprint of
Pegasus Elliot MacKenzie Publishers Ltd.
www.pegasuspublishers.com*

First Published in 2024

**Nightingale Books
Sheraton House  Castle Park
Cambridge  England**

Printed & Bound in Great Britain

**Dedication**

To my son Kien who is exactly like me in every way.

Please follow your dreams and never give up.

My name is Freya O' Sullivan, and tomorrow, I'll be eight years old. I live in the small town of Dingle, Ireland. Lots of people think of Dublin when they think of Ireland.

Dublin is about four hours from here. I know this because we drove last summer to see my cousins and it was four hours of total donkey years in the car. I don't like to read, and there was nothing to do.

For as long as I can remember, I have hated school. I hate everything about it. No one told me I would be attached to a monster for my whole life. My monster's name is Dyslexia.

Before I started school, my monster and
I were best mates. We did everything
together. We loved to draw and make up
stories. We loved to swim. When I was four,
I started surfing lessons, and my monster
came too. My parents joked that I was born
half human and half mackerel.

Everything changed the day I started kindergarten. My monster sat at the desk next to me, but no one could see him but me. All the other kids were following directions and learning how to write their names. That didn't interest me. I needed to walk around and talk to people. My monster encouraged me to do so, and I got in trouble that day.

In class, I was more of an observer than a participant. I couldn't help but notice I was far more mature than the other children my age.

Most of the time, I would go into a kind of trance, and the teacher's voice would fade. My monster and I would start planning all the details of our annual haunted house for Halloween.

I could visualize every detail in my mind down to the last headstone and where I would place it. It didn't matter it was almost a year away.

My mind was like a sieve. If information was not interesting to me, I could never remember it no matter how hard I tried. Mam and Da bought me learning flashcards, puzzles, and videos. I wanted nothing to do with them. Learning wasn't fun.

It was a chore. Everyone else remembered things, but I didn't. While everyone else was learning math, my monster and I were working on astrology predictions for the year. I was a Capricorn, and he was a Gemini. Surely, this was way more important.

The older I got, the harder school was for me. The pressure to fit in was becoming unbearable.

The one thing I was good at besides surfing was making up stories. I was naturally creative, and my imagination was endless. I especially loved scary stories.

My monster was sad I didn't want to be mates anymore. He would sit at the end of my bed at night and cry himself to sleep.

One day, the teacher wanted me to take a test. I was surprised I was the only one in my class taking it. My monster and I decided to not read the test and just fill in the circles. It was way too much to read. We had fun making patterns. It was like our secret code. When I finished, the teacher looked serious and sad.

The next day, Mam and Da explained I had something called dyslexia. My monster Dyslexia and I had problems my other classmates didn't have.

Learning right from left was hard.
Telling time was a mystery. Tying my
runners took me longer than other kids.
Reading and retaining information wasn't
easy, and I didn't enjoy reading, but I
loved picture books so that I could
make up my own stories.

Reading out loud and not reading a
word ahead was hard, and spelling words
was a nightmare. I didn't enjoy playing
games because the instructions were
hard to understand. I struggled to finish
assignments and turn in homework.

This is what it feels like to be dyslexic.

School was not designed for kids like me. Teachers had to teach everyone and couldn't slow down for me, so I fell further and further behind. It seemed hopeless.

As I looked over at my monster who was drawing a cool picture of us surfing, I thought maybe I needed to make friends with my monster again. I couldn't do this all by myself. We always had fun.
I missed him.

That night, I sat down with my monster and had a serious heart-to-heart talk. We made a magical fort using every pillow and blanket I could find. We named it Fort Truth. It was only for us creatives. It was built with equal parts of glitter, moss, feathers, and fairy dust.
We agreed to work together on a solution. There was only one person who could help us.

The legendary Black Rock Crone of Dingle.
On the edge of town was a gaff everyone
was afraid of. It stood out because it was
made of solid river rocks all painted as black
as the night. The Black Rock Crone was
rumoured to be over two hundred years old.

She had survived so long by bathing in the
moonlight and carrying acorns in her pockets.
One boy in my class said she ate eggshells
and seaweed to stay alive for centuries.
Even though I was scared of her, we needed
some serious help. If anyone could break this
curse, she could.

The next day was Saturday, so I took a long
walk with my monster and thought about
what I was going to say. When I reached the
Black Rock Crone's gaff, I was frozen with fear.
I looked at my monster, took a
deep breath, and knocked on the door.

The Black Rock Crone answered. Her hair was ghost white, her teeth were dull, probably from eating all that seaweed, and her eyes were as blue as the sea.

"My name is Freya O'Sullivan, and this is my monster Dyslexia. We've come here to ask you to break the curse of dyslexia," I blurted out.

The Black Rock Crone burst out laughing, splitting her sides. "Come in, dear, I've been waiting for you. Welcome to the Bureau of Imagination and Solutions." She smiled. "You don't want me to break the curse," she said kindly.

"Yes, I do." My monster and I were distracted looking at all the unusual things she collected.

There were birds carved out of wood that
seemed so real I expected them to fly.
We saw paintings of landscapes of the
peninsula. Gemstones were everywhere.
I was drawn to one that seemed to
glow in the dark.

"'Tis me favourite. It's moonstone.
It's connected to all things feminine.
It represents inner peace and clarity." She
handed me the stone. "What if I could
teach you some magic to help you embrace
dyslexia?" The Black Rock Crone
poured some tea.

My monster nodded with a hopeful look.

"Drink this," the crone said and
handed us the tea.
"Is it magic?" I said hopefully.
"I'm afraid it's just Irish black tea."
She smiled.

The Black Rock Crone handed me and my
monster sparkly notebooks and fancy
pens. A whistle hung from a leather
lanyard around her neck, and she blew it
as hard as she could. I nearly dropped
my tea.

"Listen up. These are the rules," she screamed.
"Rule number one. Always take a
notebook with you and two pens
in case you lose one."
My monster and I nodded.

"Rule number two. Make short-term and long-term
lists for yourself and check
them off."

SHORT-TERM LIST

- Wash black clothes.
- Feed the birds.
- Take a walk.
- Tend to the garden.
- Paint a portrait.
- Fill up the car with petrol.
- Bake some scones.

# LONG-TERM LIST

- Plan a vacation to Mexico.
- Organize my closet.
- Take a class at a community college.
- Learn a new language.
- Donate some food and clothes.
- Volunteer at the pet shelter.
- Practice yoga.

I was happy to see eating eggshells and seaweed was not on her short-term list.

"That brings me to rule number three. Always set goals for yourself. No goal is too big. And write them down. When you write in your handwriting, it's like a spell. You will be able to remember much more information."

She showed us her notebook with beautiful handwriting.

There were drawings and symbols next to some of the writing. "Anything that can help you visually remember."

My monster and I were feverishly writing everything down.
"Rule number four. Always take notes or draw them." She turned to a page in her notebook.

"This was a Spanish language class I was taking. See my notes. " She had written Spanish words with their meanings and how to say them.

"You are a creative lovely soul. Your mind
works differently than others. That doesn't
mean that you are limited. It means
you are limitless."

All of the carved wooden birds started
flying around the room. My monster held
his hand out, and a cardinal landed on it.

"Other people can't see that. Only people like
us can." The Black Rock Crone winked.
"You're dyslexic?" I asked in amazement.
"Why, yes, of course. The position of Guardian
of the Bureau of Imagination and Solutions
is only open to creatives."

"Rule number five.
Use a highlighter to highlight
important words. Highlight names, places
and things so you remember them."
"Are there more rules?"
She nodded.
"Rule number six.
Routine is your best friend."
"When you create routines for yourself,
it quiets the mind and gives you peace."

The Black Rock Crone pointed at the
grandfather clock.
"Rule number seven.
Always be fifteen minutes early for
everything if you're on time, you're late.
Being early cuts out the stress and gives
you time to prepare. Always allow time
to get lost. "
I drew a picture of a clock with rule
number seven.

"Rule number eight. Don't compare yourself
to others. You are only competing
with yourself."

"There is only one you. You are on your
journey and no one else's. Be happy for
mates when they achieve their goals, and
know that you will achieve all of your
goals in your own time."
She took a drink of her tea.

"Rule number nine. Surround yourself with
like-minded people. It's better to have a
small group of real mates than a bunch
of fakes."

"Every person has something that makes
them unique. Be kind to everyone
as you never really know what's
going on at home."
That was a good rule. I drew a picture
with this rule too.

1
2
3

"Rule number ten. Embrace your monster. You control the monster, and the monster is part of you. Your monster is your best mate and gives you a gift that is so special you would be lost without him. Your gift is a power that is endless. Never let anyone tell you you can't do something. "

The Black Rock Crone smiled. "It's not always easy living with dyslexia, but maybe life isn't meant to be so easy. We learn from failure. The rewards are so much greater when you work for something. The secret is we have more magic in us than other people. Shh, don't tell everyone.

"They will all want to be like us."

**About the Author**

Lisa Penner-Dang grew up all over the country. She hated school and reading until one day in high school a teacher gave her a Stephen King book to read. That changed everything. She learned ways to navigate her learning disabilities. She graduated with a BA in Fashion Design and Merchandising from the American College of the Applied Arts in London, England, and Los Angeles, California. Lisa worked as a photo stylist for magazines and catalogs. She is now writing screenplays and several more children's books. She is currently living in Kenai, Alaska.

Printed in the USA
CPSIA information can be obtained
at www.ICGtesting.com
CBHW062156280624
10833CB00015B/127